The (NOT) Scary Shark

Tamia Sheldon

ISBN: 978-1-68195-269-7 • eISBN: 978-1-68195-270-3 • ePib ISBN: 978-1-68195-271-0

Published in the United States by Xist Publishing www.xistpublishing.com

The sun slipped down and the moon rose above the sea. The fish and animals of the ocean grew quiet as they fell asleep.

But, deep under the sea a shark named Amelia looked around for something, anything to do.

Amelia was not sleepy.

Amelia saw her friend, May the seahorse, swimming by "Hello May," she said, "Why are you still awake?"

"I can't sleep because I'm worried about having a bad dream." said May.

"What kind of bad dream?" asked Amelia.

"Well," May sighed," I once had a bad dream that a big rock fell on my tail."

"Ohhh!" said Amelia, "That is scary. If you don't sleep near any rocks, you won't have to worry!"

"Thank you!" May said.

Amelia was still not sleepy.

Amelia heard a small voice. "I can't sleep either!" giggled a little clown fish named Jester.

"Why not?" Amelia asked.

"Because. . . because I'm thirsty." Jester looked at her and smiled.

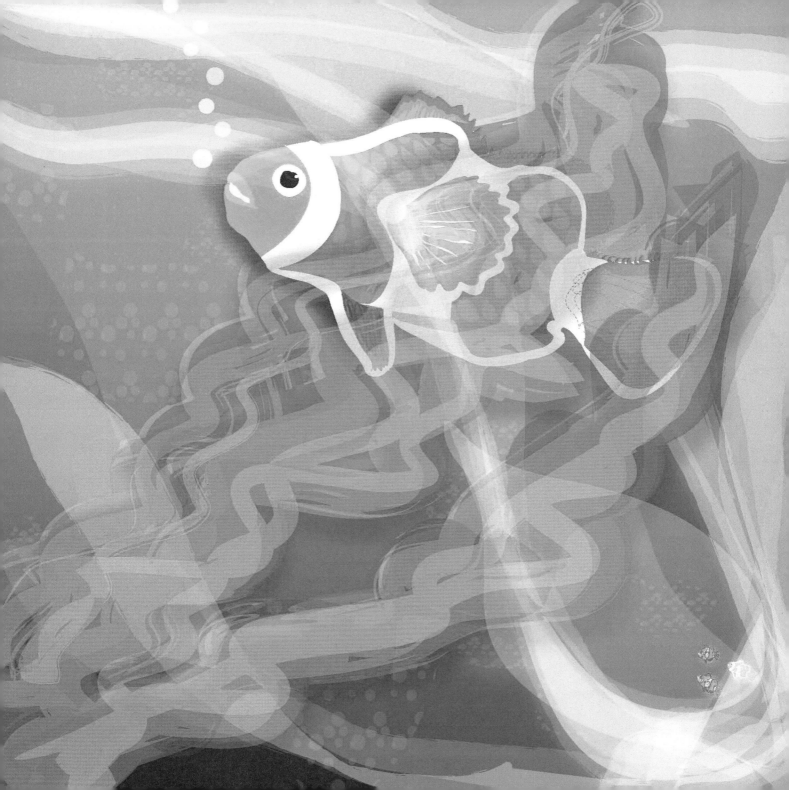

Amelia stared at the clown fish.
She was very confused,
"But...but we live in the water!" she said.

"I know!" Jester giggled. "I was just joking!"

The clown fish zipped away to find another audience for his joke.

Amelia laughed and laughed. She was definitely not sleepy.

Amelia saw Ada, who was swimming with a frown. "Hello, how are you?" Amelia asked.

Ada shivered. "I'm trying to sleep but I'm much too cold. Even when I tuck into my shell, I cannot get warm."

"Hmmm…" said Amelia, "You know,
there is a warm gulf stream near my cave.
You could go sleep there!
It would be very warm and cozy."

With a flick of her flipper, Ada replied,
"That is wonderful news! Thank you,
thank you! I'm so tired!"

Amelia was glad, but she was still not
sleepy.

"Hello Amelia" said a tiny voice.
It was Hanna, she was fanning her face
with her claws.

"What are you doing?" asked Amelia.

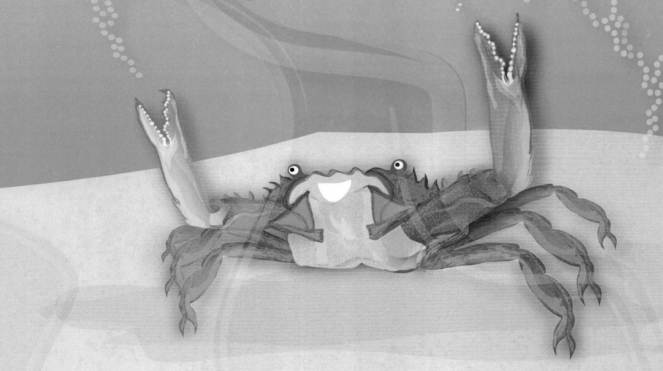

"I'm trying to cool off, I just can't sleep
because I'm too hot."

Amelia thought to herself. "Well, I just passed Ada and she said it's very cold back there. Maybe now you can sleep?"

Hanna clicked her claws and moved quickly to the cold spot.

Amelia was still not sleepy.

She saw Sasha and swam over to her,

"Hi Sasha, how come you're not sleeping tonight?"

Sasha groaned, "Because my little brother is bothering me and keeps waking me up. Every time I try to sleep he swims around and around and around me."

"Why don't you let him come snuggle with you?" Amelia grinned. "Then you can both go to sleep!"

Sasha swam away to find her brother, and Amelia was still not sleepy.

Amelia saw a large school of fish swimming quickly towards her.

"Hello!" She called, "Why are you guys still awake?"

"We're hungry! We're hungry We're hungry!" The fish swirled and shouted as they swam around Amelia.

"Oh, I know the feeling," said Amelia.

One brave fish swam forward and said "We eat krill, these itty bitty creatures and we can't seem to find any. Our whole family is hungry and tired and really, really grumpy!"

"Well," said Amelia, "What do krill look like? Hmmm…Like a small cloud in the water I suppose. Like…like that?"

Amelia pointed with her fin and all the fish screamed with joy. "DINNER!" They swam off calling, "Goodnight, thank you!"

Amelia was was still not sleepy.

Amelia said hello to her friend Olivia,
"Why are you still awake?" Amelia asked.

"There is SO MUCH to see and do! I can't sleep because I want to play and eat and swim and visit with my friends!"

Amelia agreed, "There is always something fun happening and it can be hard to fall asleep if you are afraid to miss out."

Lucy was swimming by and overheard Amelia talking. "Oh dear," she said, "You're having trouble sleeping?"

"Yes," said Amelia.

"That is horrible!" said Lucy, "Maybe you could try sleeping like I do. I fall right to sleep every night. Bedtime is my favorite time of day."

"How do you sleep?" asked Amelia.

"Well, first I wiggle my whole body and stretch out my tail. Then I stand on my head and close my eyes."

Amelia gasped. "You sleep standing on your head?"

"It's quite comfortable, you should try it."

Amelia wiggled her body, stretched her tail and flipped upside down.

"Woooooow….I feel very dizzy."

Amelia decided that sleeping on her head was not going to work, but she felt a little bit….sleepy.

Amelia felt her eyes grow heavy. Her fins were tired. She...she was tired.

Really, really tired! She swam home yawning huge yawns,

"Ahoooooo Yaaaaaaaaawn." She swam in three circles and yawned again.

All across the ocean, creatures big and small rested their bodies and minds.

In the morning, they would wake up full of energy because they had recharged and rested.

As the moon rose fully into the sky and moonlight filtered down through the deep blue water, Amelia finally went to bed.

She closed her eyes, curled her tail and fell asleep.

82276084R00024

Made in the USA
Lexington, KY
28 February 2018